T0284925

SHOOT THE STORM

ANNETTE DANIELS TAYLOR

An imprint of Enslow Publishing

WEST 44 BOOKS™

Please visit our website, www.west44books.com.
For a free color catalog of all our high-quality books,
call toll free 1-800-398-2504.

Cataloging-in-Publication Data

Names: Daniels Taylor, Annette.
Title: Shoot the storm / Annette Daniels Taylor.
Description: New York : West 44, 2022. | Series: West 44
YA verse
Identifiers: ISBN 9781978595576 (pbk.) | ISBN
9781978595675 (library bound) | ISBN 9781978595590
(ebook)
Subjects: LCSH: Children's poetry, American. | Children's
poetry, English. | English poetry.
Classification: LCC PS586.3 D365 2022 | DDC
811'.60809282--dc23

First Edition

Published in 2022 by
Enslow Publishing LLC
29 East 21st Street
New York, NY 10011

Editor: Caitie McAneney
Designer: Tanya Dellaccio

Photo Credits: Cover (main image) krsmanovic/
Shutterstock.com.

Printed in the United States of America

CPSIA compliance information: Batch #CW22W44: For further information contact
Enslow Publishing LLC, New York, New York at 1-800-398-2504.

*For Rodney, who taught me
heart and hustle and basketball.*

DAD CALLS ME DOUBLE-A

My name is Aaliyah Davis.
Dad says, *Ballers need an alias,
like a superhero or a rapper.*
Double-A, mine.

I'M FOUR

Dad's locked up.
Says,
My choices
didn't pay off.
Sometimes honor's all you got.
I'll make it up to you
one day.
Wait on me,
Double-A.
We'll be that in-real-life
dad and daughter
soon.

I'M SIX

Mom tells me, Granma, and Pop-Pop
she needs a change of scenery.
I'm watching Pop-Pop.
He's putting our suitcases in the trunk.
Waving goodbye.
Mom hits the horn twice.
Hollering to the sky,
driving to Atlanta,
talking 'bout warm weather.

LOST IN THE WOODS

Remember Hansel and Gretel?
Dropping breadcrumbs for escape trails
out in the woods.
They get back home.
How I'mma make a trail from the car?
Breadcrumbs just float on the wind.
How Daddy gonna find us, Mom?

She gives me a side-eye glance.

> *Girl, please. I'm free!*

Her answer to me.

HEAT, HUMIDITY, AND HOTLANTA

Mom loving Atlanta.
Atlanta Wayne's home.
Wayne loving Mom.
Mom loving Wayne's car.
Wayne gotta son.
Dwayne his name.
Dwayne is five.
His mom dead.
My mom making future plans.
Wayne makin' plans, too.
I just wanna stop sweatin'.
Maybe make a friend at school.

THIS STEPDAUGHTER

don't like Wayne.
Wayne don't like me none neither.
Mom says,
Just act right.
Stay out of sight.
Babysit Dwayne when we out at night.

WHEN I'M TEN

Everything changes, again.
Wayne tryna play me.
Like,

> *Janeen, you sure this **your** daughter?*
> *Don't even look like you.*
> *She all muscles,*
> *always looking hard.*

Mom don't defend.
The way *I* look don't *work* for her.
Sucking her teeth, she says,

> *She always been her daddy's son.*

SOLUTIONS

I'm a problem for solving.
Mall shopping.
Beauty-salon sitting.
My hair, my nails.
My clothes?
Is the outside a problem?
Dresses, skirts, floral jumpsuits.
Earrings, lip gloss, pumps.
Even church.
Arguments happening.
Wayne and Mom.
Mom and me.
Plans are made.
Phone calls, messages.
Suitcases packed.

MOM SENDS ME BACK

to Granma and Pop-Pop.
Dad's parents.

They have a little restaurant,
Miss Mary's Dinette.
Pop-Pop named it after Granma.
It's bright and sunny
like her.
We live upstairs.
Granma says
Dad looks like Pop-Pop,
I look like Dad.
Tall, broad, chocolatey skin, tar-black
hair.

FOUR A.M.

Alarm is Granma singing.
Five o'clock:
Pop-Pop's feet
hammer downstairs.
Prepping customers' breakfasts.
Six o'clock:
Granma's solo sung in my room.
Six fifteen:
I'm out the shower.
Six forty-five:
Downstairs eating breakfast.
Seven o'clock:
Granma opens the doors.
Seven-o-five:
Customers order today's special.

WHEN DAD GOT HOME

I was 11.
Now, I'm 16.
He keeps the promise,
in-real-life Dad.
Teaches me ball.
Everything he knows.
Makes me strong.
Makes me outlast anyone on the court.
Makes me run relays,
back and forth.
I'm tired—
        —Don't stop!

I KNOW WHAT MOM MEANT

...she her daddy's son!
Ain't make me mad.
Or happy.
Dad gets me.
Like my braids, we entwined.
Not his daughter, or girly-girl.

His child.

We walk the hood, folks ask,

Yo, that's you?

Dad smiles, looks me over, saying,

You know it!

Then,

Yo, that's what's up!

DAD WISDOM

Your hands are tools
for building, climbing,
touching, holding, catching,
and throwing.
The ball's yours,
power in hand,
make the decision.
Fast thinking,
for the team, for the win.
Champions ain't basic.
Be a champion.

Always do the work.

Sharing dap, I agree.
His hand with my hand.

Clap, slide, finger-grab, snap, bump, fly!

DAD GOT OUTTA PRISON

with a college degree.
Granma happy.
Say,
Used your time wisely, Georgie.

Pop-Pop say,

> *Stay away from corner trouble.*
> *You hear?*
> *Five years! Five years, for what?*
> *Where those boys at now?*

Pop-Pop getting Granma in it.

> *Mary, they come by here?*

Granma answer,

Theo, you know they ain't!

> *Son, don't forget.*
> *We all we got.*
> *We take care of each other.*

STARTING

on McKinley High's girls' basketball
team.
Dad says I'm growing into my own.
At five foot ten, I'm hard to ignore.
Basketball's my love.
I love basketball.
Basketball loves me.
We're good together.
Working me in the morning.
Tucking me in at night.
Orange rubber ball.
Traveling.
Asphalt playgrounds.
Oak gym floors.
Concrete sidewalks.
We call next!

I'M THE

Double A-
L-I-Y-A-H.
Wear the crown.
Double-A got aim.
I'm "A" dash "1."
I can hold it down!

My daddy, he learned me.
Now I got game.
My teammates, they for me.
We roll deep in this game.

Double-A got ya back.
Quick pass.
Fast break.
Double-A, we on track
to rule this game!

WHEN DAD'S HOME

he volunteers
at the Community Center.
Center director's Miss Sheree.

She and Dad got together
before he got with Mom.
Mom got pregnant,
with me.

Miss Sheree went to college.

Miss Sheree gave Dad a job,
Community Coordinator.
He handles problems.

He like it.
He like her.
She like him, too.

MS. HENDERSON DON'T LIKE ME

She has it out for me.

Always close talking.
Always coffee-breath smelling.
Always threatening me.

Tell me to write this.
Tell me to write that.
Tell me I'mma lose privileges.
Tell me basketball a privilege.

Ms. Henderson don't know—
nobody benching the star player!

PAPA DON'T TAKE NO MESS

Double-A, you making excuses.
End that!
Do what you supposed to!

But!

Don't interrupt!

You wrong. Ms. Henderson right.
You strong,
squash the fight.

Change your attitude,
Ms. Henderson in charge.
You being rude.

The team made of five.

Pass the class or get benched.
Drop the ego, lose your pride.

WATCHING CHAMPIONS

Do better work.
You know you can.
I got your back,
you got my hands.
Bring those grades up.
Some As and Bs!
We'll take a dream trip,
high up above the trees.
Summertime airplane flight.
Where WNBA All-Stars
play under lights.
You do the work.
I'll lay the plan.
We'll watch your favorite players
become champions!

SATURDAY I'M AWAKE EARLIER THAN EARLY

Before working the restaurant,
we go over missed assignments.
Dad makes a new afterschool schedule.
Can't play ball until finished.
English and social studies,
the two classes I hate.
Always asking me to write.
Dad's a good writer.
Never noticed that.
Dad reads my writing out loud.
Sounds better that way.

I ASK HIM

How you get good writing and reading?
Talking stuff Ms. Henderson be teaching.

> *I was locked up.*
> *What I'mma do?*
> *Reading, writing with prison college?*
> *Or jail education in*
> *gangster knowledge?*
> *Knowing these streets,*
> *I choose to climb, to reach!*
>
> *Basketball's good for body and mind.*
> *But Black folks need more*
> *for this grind.*

BACK IN THE DAY

Everyone called my Dad
Boogie-G.
Granma don't allow Dad being called
Boogie-G.
Granma says,

> That's a gang name.
> George free now!
> Only slaves go by a master's name.
> Take back the name I gave you!

WE WATCHING NETFLIX

Dad coming out his room.
Ooh, you look nice, Dad!
New kicks?
When'd you go shopping?
        (sniff, sniff)
You wearing cologne?

Dad say,
        Why you all up in my business?

Pop-Pop say,
        Who's the lucky lady, Georgie?

Granma say,
        Georgie, you finally ask Sheree out?
        She's a nice girl. I always liked her!

A 65-DEGREE FEBRUARY DAY

Weird warm winter weather miracle!
Mid-winter break!
Everybody out of school.
Community Center is full.
Dad opens the outdoor court
for three-on-three game.
Devonte, Me, and Jerel
versus Jada, Nikki, and Micah.
Jada plays dirty.
Got Jerel's back
on the rebound.
Turn to see Dad.
Not looking at me.
Hopping off the bleachers.

BEFORE ANYONE
KNOWS ANYTHING

we hear a familiar sound.
On the east side of Buffalo,
you've heard it before.

At first, I tell myself,
it's a firecracker.
 I know it's not,
 but that's what I tell myself.
Until I hear another
and another.

 Now I know.

Now everyone else knows.

Now everyone else runs.

 Except me.

THEY'RE SCREAMING AND RUNNING

I'm stuck. I'm staring.
I don't know what's coming.
I don't think I'm breathing.

My legs aren't running.
My mouth cannot speak.
My dad's on the ground.

What's happening to me?

> *Dad, can you hear me?*

My lips aren't moving.

> *Dad, can you hear me?*

His body is bleeding.

> *Dad, please get up!*
> *Dad, please don't leave me.*

MISS SHEREE CALLS
THE AMBULANCE

Granma and Pop-Pop
at the hospital.
Miss Sheree's blouse is red
from Dad's blood.
Her hands shake and hold me.

Police ask me questions.
What did you see?

I stare,
no answers.
Pop-Pop is yelling,

She's in shock!

Feeling a shock like—
like electricity buzzing?
Feeling it.
All over my body.

AT THE FUNERAL

Lots of people sit.
Lots of people cry.
Paying respects.
To Dad.
To me.

Who are you??

They speak.
Say sorry.
Say, *Anything you need...*
Say, *I remember...*

Who are you???

Telling stories,
they cry.
Miss Sheree cries.
Granma cries.
Pop-Pop frowns.
I'm nothin'.
Say nothin'.
Feel nothin'.

MOM AND WAYNE

come up with Dwayne.
Mom and Granma talking.
Granma says,

> *Janeen, it's too soon!*
> *It's not the place.*

Well when, Mary?
She's my daughter!

> *Got some nerve talking, your daughter!*
> *You left her for another man!*
> *George's body ain't even cold yet.*

I don't want her to end up like George!

MOM AND WAYNE WAS WHISPERIN'

Least, they thought they was whisperin'.

You know, he just got out...

That's a shame...

*Always happening to brothas
tryna do right...*

Yo, I hear Boogie-G was back in...

Where you hear dat...?

That's why they popped him...

Nah, Boogie-G straight...

Well, that's what I heard...

Well, you heard wrong...

TIME TO GO

Walking out the door.

Nobody notices.

I'm running up Jefferson Avenue.
Passing the library.
Passing the *Challenger News* office.
Passing Family Dollar.
Passing Tops Friendly Markets.
Passing the fire station.
To Johnny B. Wiley Stadium.
        I run, I run, I run.
        Wanting to fly.
        Hoping my feet lift with the wind.

        Needing my feet to take me

           Away.

YO, DOUBLE-A, WHA'S UP?

Eyes opening.
Jada standing over me.
> *You good?*
I sit up.
She sits down.

> *Yo, Aaliyah, man.*
> *Yeah, sorry 'bout ya dad.*
> *Sorry I cut out.*
> *Not the ending he deserve.*
> *He was mad cool.*

We sit
for a long time.
Not saying nothing.
We sit.
The sun goes down.

MISS SHEREE VISITS

Granma say I still not talkin'.

Miss Sheree says,
Maybe we should take her to a doctor?

    Granma say,
    Aaliyah sad. I'm sad, too.
    Shoot, Pop-Pop act like everything
    the same.

That's why we should take Aaliyah to see a
doctor, Miss Mary.
She did more than lose George.
She watched him die.

    Hmph, we'll go to church.

HAVEN'T BEEN TO CHURCH SINCE

Dad's funeral.
When Dad was home,
I only come here
Easter, Mother's Day,
Granma's birthday,
Christmas Eve.

Church full a
Miss Coras, Miss Sherees
Miss Lisas, with their kids,
standing 'round me.

Pastor Gorham lay hands on me.
Praying hard.
Face dripping.
Hope God hear him soon.

Wanna leave.
Wanna run.

POP-POP CALLS ME

to watch TV.
He points to
a box of DVDs and notebooks.

These were your dad's.
Rapping and basketball.
He was good at both.
I know you miss him.
I know you angry.
I'm mad too.
Maybe these help you
get your voice back.

PRESS PLAY

Young Dad with a mic!
On stage at Juneteenth,
Dad with flow
moving the crowd!

Next clip, Dad's in a
McKinley High uniform. Layup!
Next clip,
Dad celebrating with the team.

For a few minutes,

I forget.

That Dad is gone.
Shot.
Killed.
Dead.

THE VIDEO ENDS

Dad is not here.
Or anywhere.
He's only on these videos.

His voice stops.
Sound passes through.
Out my lips.
Why?

Looking toward the ceiling.

WHY?! WHY?!

My long feet kick over the box.
Notebooks fall out.
One is black, hardcovered,
pebbly, and thick.
Thumbing through, it's filled.
With Dad's handwriting.
Rhymes and verses.

"FELL IN LOVE"

With Janeen.
She was fine,
Mmm, Janeen.
Looking like a queen.

Janeen started changing.
Start feeling like a stranger.
Pushing me into danger.
So, she can ride a Mustang.

Start slinging that rock.
Another brotha on the block.
Tryna be what he not.
To keep the love that he got.

For Janeen.

"BABY MAKES FAMILY"

What you do
when your woman tells you
baby coming soon?
What you do
when joyful news turns sad?
What you do
when your woman tells you
married life need cash?
How you act
when life change paths?

Gonna make a plan.
Gonna take a stand.
Gonna be that man.
Gonna get that gun.
Gonna do them runs.
Gonna get that cheese.

So, me and mine eat.

MAKING A PLAN

Cry in private.
Can't show the pain.
Try to recollect.
This ain't no dream.

Hoping it's a nightmare.
But can't wake up.
Revenge is like a taste for blood.
Want a full cup.

How can I honor
my dad's legacy?

A plan.
What I'm thinking.
Vengeance I'll be drinking.

Find the killer.
Turn him to victim.

In the grave
sinking.

NEVER FORGET
FAMILY FIRST

Fruit seeds planted.
Sorrow like a curse.

Like you, Dad,
I'm gonna get a gun.
I'm gonna find the one.

Your legit life,
took your last breath.
Bullet's named for you.
Now, what we got left?

Bullets for bullets.
Eye for eye.
Soon and soon
that killer gonna die.

Find a gun.

42

COACH'S TALK

How're you doing?
What happened to your dad was foul.
I lost my dad when I was
about your age.
Stroke.
If you need an ear to listen,
she says,
I got two.

Something grows inside my throat.
My mouth opens, letting words come out.

I'm okay.
The words croak from between my lips.

Resting hands on my shoulders,
Coach adds,
It's alright, if you're not.

My eyes begin stinging.
They overfill.
I sit with the tissues she hands me.

BASKETBALL PRACTICE

Practice
don't feel the same.
Where's purpose?
Lost some sweetness
for the game.
Did it leave with Dad?

Feeling half empty.
Coach says, *Grief causes distraction.*
She says, *Team is family.*
Working and communicating,
together, makes this game.

Not feeling teammates.
Not feeling togetherness.
Feeling muscle memory.

On the court.
No thinking.
Reaction.
Ball in my hands.
Feeling anger.

I do
what I know.

JADA WAVE ME OVER

Walking with my lunch tray.
Her crew got the way-back corner table.
By the staircase and girls' bathroom.

Laughing, clowning all day.

At my locker,
Jada and some big dude, sliding over.

You know Lou?
Dis Aaliyah!

Heavy-eyed Lou.
Yawning.

What up...my condolences.

I nod my thanks.

AFTER PRACTICE

Coach says,
Next game, you'll be the sixth man.

But I'm ready!
I say, *I got this!*

> *Aaliyah,*
> **Coach says,**
> *the sixth man is important.*
> *You could replace Lisette,*
> *Gigi, or Brianna!*
> *Who else can play Center,*
> *Guard, Forward?*

Nobody but me!

> *Exactly.*
> *You're the sixth man.*
> *Two more games til finals!*

LEAVING THE GYM

Yo, Aaliyah, hold up!

Jada's waiting on me.

Let's hang out.
Like, I like the way you…
You cool, Aaliyah.
You know?
I thought…
Was thinking…
We could hang?
Shoot hoops?
I don't know.
You like other stuff?
You like music?
I like you.
That's all.

I like you.

YOU GETTING ON THIS BUS?

I like Jada, know what I mean?
She's cool and all.
I wasn't looking at her
that way.
She cute though,
    but she rough.

Like tree bark and sandpaper.
We laughing though.

I like that.

On the bus, we crack up.
Later, I don't know why.

KNOW SOME FOLKS HERE

We walking through
Forest Lawn Cemetery.

Jada says,
Few family.
Few friends.
You scared?

No.
Looks like a park.

Yeah, that's why I like it.

My mom gonna bury me here.
Right next to my daddy.
We got the plot.
Space all ready.
They fit six of us in one spot!

I probably won't make
it to twenty-five.

WHY YOU SAY THAT?

Jada explains,

> Most my family dead before thirty.
>
> My daddy, three cousins, a brother,
> two uncles, an auntie.
> That's why I'm always packing.

Jada shows me a gun.

> Jada "Un-play-wit-able!" they call me.

She says,
> If I'm going out, we gonna
> light everything up!
> Hill Street Crew don't take
> no prisoners!
> Nobody got time for that!

YOU WANNA GUN?

Jada asks me, like she's joking.

Word?
I say, serious.

> *I thought you was Miss Goody-Goody.*
> *Baller Queen Bee.*
> *What you gonna do with a piece?*
> *You know who killed your dad?*
> *Then how you gonna hit him?*
> *You need a plan.*
>
> *I know a man.*
> *My godfather.*
> *He gonna hook you up!*

LAND-LORD

Who Jada's talking about:
Six foot two, smooth.
Toothpick resting
side of mouth.

Looking like he just left the barbershop.
Edge-up.
Sharp.
"L-L" edged in his fade.

New "LeBrons" on his feet.
Apple Watch on his wrist.

He the real deal,
nothing fake about him.

Know why he called Land-Lord?
Cause he own these streets.

I KNOW YOU

Land-Lord says.

Know your people, too.
Boogie-G, Janeen?
Mhmm.
Yeah, we rolled deep back in the day.
Your mama
was my girl
first.

Hearing his
first
feels funny
in my stomach.

Office in the back of his car repair shop.
Don't dress like nobody's mechanic
though.

So, who you trying to off?

WHOEVER KILLED MY FATHER

You know who that is?

No.

Oh, you 'bout to be Sherlock Holmes.
Jada, that make you Watson, huh?

Didn't come for jokes.
Came for merchandise.

Hold up. My condolences.
But, in this business, "merchandise"
ain't free.

How much?

He's grinning, while his eyes feel
me out.
I got several income streams,
Land-Lord says.
Fixing and tricking out cars.
Speculating on sports, doing favors.

Selling guns? I say.

Yeah, and other things,
Land-Lord says.
Jada, you carrying?

Jada pulls up her sweatshirt.
Black handle with a bit of silver sits
inside her belt.
I try not to look surprised.

Count on Jada for...
assistance.
Pass it to her, Jada.
Let her hold it.

I take the weapon.
Feels heavy.

This one's got power.
Feels good, huh?
Try this out.

He shows me a different one.

This one's lightweight, easy to conceal.
Maybe more your style?
Semiautomatic, under a pound.

YOU AIN'T ANSWER ABOUT PRICE

I say.

> Land-Lord says,
> *Naw, I didn't.*

He hands me the second gun.
It's black and tan.

> *Hold this.*

It's lighter.

> *Yeah.*
> *Feel good?*

Mmhm.

I feel stronger
holding it.
Invincible, even.
I aim at the desk.

HOLD ON, NOW!

Don't shoot me!
You need lessons.
Jada, go to the back.
Pirate'll set you up.

Then,
Double-A,
I'll dig for you.
Solve your mystery.
Now, you owe me.

What's the fee?

Don't worry,
you can afford it.
You still starting?

Nah, second string.

That's alright.
I'll send my invoice
soon.

WHY YOU START CARRYING?

I ask Jada.

Jada looks up at me before answering.

> *Daddy shot dead.*
> *Buying my birthday cake.*
> *Jamal shot dead.*
> *Walking home late.*
> *Laron shot dead.*
> *Locking up his bike.*
> *YOUR daddy shot dead.*
> *In broad daylight.*
> *Junie shot dead.*
> *Ordering pizza.*
> *Jasmine shot dead.*
> *Never ever gonna see her.*
>
> *Now we both loading up.*
> *Ready to shoot*
> *one more up!*

THE DUSTY
CORNER STORE

Anything not
sweet, chewy, crispy, or salty
is dusty.

Thick bulletproof plexiglass
protects employees.
Little pass-throughs
for money & merch.

Cashier looking from
platform stands,
watching you.

Mostly sell
soda, candy, chips, snack cakes,
malt liquor, beer, cigarettes.

ID?
Unnecessary.

Cash & **E**lectronic**B**enefit**T**ransaction.
Jada buys two
fruit-flavored malt liquors.

To get lit.

WE SIT ON THE BENCH

The Moselle Street
basketball court.

Sipping fake strawberry.
Holding cold cans.
Jada slurs telling her story.

> *Yo, I'm four years old*
> *when my pops got shot.*
> *Land-Lord help Mom.*
> *Made sure we ate.*
> *Just know this life ain't long.*
> *So, I want mine comfortable.*
> *I owe Land-Lord.*
> *He stepped up for mine.*

SOMETIMES WHEN I'M DREAMING

it plays all over again.
On the court.
With you and the others.
My dad walks out.
Dude walks up.
Hoodie up.
Covering his face.
Dad looks.
Dude raises his hand.
Bam, bam, bam.

> *See his face?*
> **Jada asks.**

Never really clear.

> *Nothing happens*
> *without Land-Lord knowing.*

> *We gonna see his face soon.*

WHAT TIME YOU GET HOME?

Granma bust the door open.
Lights all on.
I answer,
Don't know.

> *I know.*
> *One-thirty in the a.m.*
> *Who do you think you are?*

If you already knew, why did you ask me?

> *Girl, watch your mouth!*

Rolling over.
Kissing my pillow.
I'm sick.
Granma snatches covers.
Hey! I don't feel good!

YOU AIN'T GROWN

Get your butt up!
Wash your sweat off!
Get downstairs,
prep for breakfast!
Then get to school!
You better be home by five o'clock.
You got a date with a mop!

Sitting up, sucking my teeth
gets me a smack on my head.

You better mind yourself,
Miss Aaliyah!
I'm not the one!
Pop-Pop stuck in his head.
You running the streets.
I'm not having this in my house!

I HIDE THE GUN

inside a Nike shoebox,
back of my closet.

Falling asleep in Ms. Henderson's class,
she clowning me
in front of everybody.

Asking,
You want a blanket and a pillow?

I say, *Yeah.*
And a back massage.
A lullaby.

Then,
I stand up.
Bend over.

And a goodnight kiss…

Laughter roars!

THAT'S ENOUGH, MISS DAVIS!

she says,
turning red as a Twizzler.

Now you mad?
I say.
You took the shot.
Not my fault you fouled out!

Classroom laughs.

Teacher's weapon:
> *Your behavior is unacceptable.*
> *Go to the office right away!*

If I get one more detention,
I could miss a game.

LEAVING DETENTION

Heavy-eyed Lou in there, too.

> **Nods,**
> *What's up?*

You see Jada?

> *Nah,*
> **he says.**
> *She absent.*
> *Land-Lord sent her on a run.*

What you do for Land-Lord, Lou?

> *I'm a bridge.*
> *Go to school*
> *to bridge connections.*
> *Buyers with merchandise.*
> *Kids got money without bills.*
> *They always wanting something.*

LATE FOR PRACTICE

I have to run drills.
Coach Barron gives me a lecture.

You wanna start again?
Don't get pulled into
Ms. Henderson's traps.

She just don't like me.

Exactly.
So don't agitate her.
We have two games to the playoffs!
You get another detention,
you'll miss one of those games!

JADA MEETS UP

Hands over a bag.
Gives a shake.
Sounds like a rattlesnake.
Small beige pills
in an amber bottle.

> *Land-Lord says*
> *take one every day.*
> *I'm supposed to make sure*
> *you take one.*
> *So, the next games,*
> *you'll dominate*
> *to get to the finals!*

Nothing wrong with
my game.
Always dominate!

JADA MAKES A CASE

In practice you been strugglin'.
I been watching you.
Last game you stop hustlin'.
That's truth.
Ain't playin' the same.
Lost heart for game.
Ain't startin' no more.
Here, making complaints
and dealing with "Land-Lord."

Hurry and swallow it down,
easy and quick.
Ain't got time for all this!

WE ABOUT TO THROW DOWN

When the illest
olive-green Lexus LX SUV
pulls up.
Beep-beeping.

Tinted window rolling down.
Revealing Land-Lord.

Let me take you home.

Nah,
I say.
Bus be here.

Get in.

Sucking my teeth.
We get in.
Me in front,
Jada in back.

World feels and
sounds different
inside this whip.

Looking up,
I see the sky!

IF HEAVEN
WAS A RIDE

It would feel like this.

Like it?

Nice.
Smells good,
I say.

New car smell.
I'm about enjoying
the fruits of labor.

She won't take the pills,
Jada says.

Think I'm about messing you up?
Done seen Jekyll and Hyde.
He laughs.
You'll just be a beast on the court!

ALREADY A BEAST, DON'T WANNA BE NO MONSTER

I tell him.

> Land-Lord says,
> *Jada hasn't learned*
> *how to communicate.*
> *They're natural supplements.*
> *Ain't gonna hurt.*
> *Take 'em or not,*
> *but they'll enhance performance.*
> *So, Double-A, you an eleven?*

Huh?

> *Your feet. Shoes. Eleven?*

Yeah?
How you know?

> *I'm a man of many gifts.*
> *Jada, pass the kicks up.*

RED-AND-WHITE NIKE BOX

Pulling crisp crackly
white tissue paper.
New gray Kobe ADs.

An orange swoosh.
Size 9½ men's = 11 women's.

These two-hundred-dollar shoes?

Double-A,
consider our relationship
a partnership.
Supplements, kicks,
your gun.
Community investments.
Helping you,
kids like you
succeed.
Eliminating distractions by
searching for your enemy.

WHAT ABOUT MY DEBT?

I ask.

> You all business, huh?
> Hmph, just like your mama.

He stares through me a minute.

> Take the supplements.
> Enjoy the shoes.
> Don't be late for practice.
> Get McKinley to the finals.
>
> Help your g-ma.
> Don't give them trouble.
>
> I hear your grand-pops
> wake up with a hangover
> since the funeral.
>
> Family first.

HOW YOU IN MY BUSINESS?

Told you, a partnership.

The car stops
a block from home.
4:45 p.m.

Shoes in backpack without a box.
Granma would ask questions.

Jada, standing between
the car's front and back door.

> *Yo, Aaliyah.*
> *My bad.*
> *Shouldn'tve pushed up on you*
> *like that.*

Jada sticks out a hand.

SMACKING JADA'S HAND AWAY

Bending my knees, a little,
wrapping arms around her waist.
Squeezing her tight.
Lifting
up.

What you doing?!

Yelling from above.

Yo! Put me down!

*Hurry kissing and
making up already,*
Land-Lord says,
I got business.

Tell me who dominates on the court?

Huh?

Who dominates?

You do!

Say my name, girl!

*Double-A!
Aaliyah Davis
dominates the court!*

YOU WANNA HANG OUT?

I ask her.

Jada looks at Land-Lord
for permission.

> He says,
> *Go ahead, catch up later.*

We walk.
Then I remember Granma and chores.

*Yo, I forgot, I'm gonna have to do some
chores when I get home.*

> *That's okay, I'm down.
> Think I could get a free slice
> of your Granmama's pie?*

WHAT KINDA PIE?

It don't matter, **Jada says.**
Whatever she bakes is good!
Does she bake in the house?
Like when you not selling it?

My Granma don't bake the pies.
She buys them from a lady
who got a bakery over on Walden Avenue.
She makes the banana puddings, though.
Baking takes lotta time!

GLAD I DIDN'T HAVE TO GO SEND FOR YOU

Granma says.
*Didn't say you could
have company.*

This Jada,
I tell her.

*As long as she don't keep you
from chores.
Your mama knows you here?*
Granma asks Jada.

No, ma'am.

You make sure you call her.

Granma turns to me.
*Had a conversation with your
English teacher.*

Ms. Henderson?

*Called about you being foolish.
You're getting tutoring
right away!*

BUT GRANMA!

*I'm gonna pay Miss Cora's
Shanequa to tutor you.*

*Ain't got time for Shanequa's books!
I got practice!
And...*

And what?

She looks at Jada.
*Don't get all smart because of
your little friend.*

I'm not.
I am embarrassed.

*Been acting like "I don't
know what"
since Georgie been, been...*

*Killed?
Shot?
Dead?*

NOT SAYING IT
DON'T DO NOTHING

Might as well say it.

Somebody.
Some human.
Some person.

Walked.
Right up.

Three bullets.
Ran away.

So, yeah.
Mop floors.
Remove trash.
School attendance.
Practice.

As usual.
But
George Davis Jr.
was murdered.

His killer is still breathing.

Saying it.
Not saying it.
Doing good.
Doing bad.
Don't change nothing.

BUT I DON'T SAY THAT

I just think it.

> Your grandfather
> uses that word.
> I don't like it!

She whispers,
Dead.
Why y'all gotta talk negative?

Negative?

> Your daddy passed.
> That's what you say.
> Passed.

Passed?
What did he pass?
A test?
Was Murder the test?
Did he pass us by?
Like a breeze in summer?

KEEP IT INSIDE

It's not worth the argument.
Because that's what will happen.
Granma doesn't understand
my anger.

She doesn't wanna understand.
Doesn't want us to be angry.
Her knees on overtime.
Praying for strength, courage,
and wisdom.

Pop-Pop can't understand.
Lately, he's too busy practicing
a magic act
to make himself disappear.

CAN WE GO NOW?

Long as you know to meet
Shanequa tomorrow!
Granma says.

I keep my face blank
so Granma can't accuse me of anything else.
She leaves us alone.

Does your mother do stuff like that?
I ask Jada.

> *Like, asking me questions?*

Like, nag you?

> *Most times, I don't even*
> *see my mother.*
> *She works three jobs.*
> *They all part time, her shifts*
> *be changing.*

MY SISTER JEWEL

Jada tells me,
Nineteen, she got two babies,
Nina and Sean.
She's in online college.
Gonna be a nurse.
Between the two of us and my ma
we take care of each other
and the twins.
And Jerel and Jermaine, they're ten.
I like your house.
I like your grandparents.
Wish mine was home.

I'M GOING OUT

Pop-Pop's new-found phrase:
I'm going out.

> Translation:
> *Don't even ask.*

I'm going out.

> Pop-Pop traveling
> up to Mike's Place.

I'm going out.

> *Back later tonight.*

I'm going out.

> Hear him staggering, stumbling.
> Falling, flopping on the couch.
> Perfumed well with
> cigarettes and rum,
> crying and moaning.

About murder.
About sons.

DAYS PASS

Pay Shanequa, but ditch
tutoring.
Instead, take one pill daily.
First, nothing different.
A week,
I feel stronger. Feel alert.

Hope what Land-Lord said
is true.

Is he really gonna find the one
I'm looking for?

Can I pay the invoice he's gonna send?

Is Jada...
            for me?
Herself?
            Or him?

Does any of it matter

            if I win?

WHEN POP-POP DOESN'T DRINK

Teaches bike riding.
Teaches bike fixing, too.

Sits cheering my team.
Sits cheering for me.
My Pop-Pop.

Wakes early for lake fishing.
Buys wiggly red-crawlers, asleep under ice.
He drives.
We laughing.
We baiting crawlers on hooks.
He smiles.
Sharing, showing.

Catching fish.
Cleaning fish.
Cooking fish.
Eating fish.

Together.

SUN STREAMS
THROUGH

the dinette windows.
Sugar, salt, and pepper
been refilled.
Coffee filters filled.
Flatware wrapped in napkins.
Potatoes and onions prepped.
Granma steady looking at me,
cross-armed.

What's the matter?

      Your muscles getting bigger?

I dunno, guess.

      Why?

I'm a baller, Granma.
Gotta work out!

GOOD NEWS TRAVELS

You going to championship!
Why you ain't tell nobody?

Pop-Pop walks in from the kitchen.

Aaliyah!
Why I heard from outside
after tonight be
finals?

When I'm supposed to tell you?
Before you leave for Mike's Place,
or after you passed out on the couch?

Granma says,
Be respectful!
He's your grandfather!

SORRY, I AIN'T SHOWED UP

to any games lately.
You know...it's, uh...

I say,
It's all good.

It's not.
Else you wouldn't have said...
Nothing's good.

Granma interrupts,
Not time to be getting into this!

Just got rage.
Anger. Inside.
Pop-Pop points to his heart.

Don't know...

Eyes already red
as fists meet wall.

GRANMA
CALLS BOBBY

See if he can
come in early.
Bobby cooks lunch.

Pop-Pop's hand gets iced.

I go to school,
thinking
one person is
responsible for all of this.

Ten blocks til the bus stop.

> Land-Lord pulls up.
> *You already missed the bus.*
> *Found who you been looking for.*
>
> *After the game,*
> *we'll have introductions.*

LEAVING THE LOCKER ROOM

Family hugging.
Fathers and mothers
kissing.

Dad, this is Aaliyah!
Brianna says.
She plays Center.
We've played together since
junior basketball camp.

We take pictures.
Her dad congratulates me.

My condolences for your father,
he adds.
He looks around
for *my family.*

I want to say,
Yeah, Brianna's dad,
I ain't got nobody.

You're invited for pizza and wings with us!

That's when I see
Jada, Heavy-eyed Lou, and
Land-Lord.

MY PEOPLE

Jada nods me over.

I say,
Thanks, but
I see my people.

Land-Lord gives me a
pound.
I knew you had that!

Jada talking with her hands.
Bow down, Queen Aaliyah!
You a BEAST!
The alley-oop
in the third!

She rained on them.

Nah, more like thunderstorm!

Brianna's people start to leave.
Her dad giving Land-Lord
a look.

WE GOT A PROBLEM?

Land-Lord turns to Brianna's dad.
The question was barely
loud enough to hear.
But we all heard.
Jada and Heavy-eyed Lou
stand straighter.
Staring.

Nah, man, I'm cool.

*Good. You looking
like I owe you money.*

Sir Land-Lord smiles.
Smooth, sure, satisfied.

He laughs.
Brianna's dad laughs.

We all laugh.

Settling away
    from afraid.

SOON AND VERY SOON

Jada, Lou, and me
with Land-Lord.

Land-Lord says,
Got what I promised.

You found out who did it?

Ready to end this?

I nod.
He turns his iPhone.

My man Digger acquired this.
Everybody didn't run.
Somebody stopped and
pressed record.

Land-Lord plays video of
Boogie-G getting shot.

The shooter's face:
clear.

RUNNING IN MY VEINS

I feel pepper
through my skin.
Waving through
and within.
Been waiting for this message.
Getting sick in this Lexus.
The killer got a face.
Land-Lord got the trace.
The clock's about to stop.
Gonna have to take the shot
before the buzzer rings.

Spill some blood.
End this thing.

WE DRIVE OUT

near the river.
Car rolls over gravelly driveway
into the building.
Moonlight reflects
on the water.

Three lights from the ceiling.
The dude sits tied to chair.
Digger and Pirate
stand guard.

There's your mark.
Have a look.

I step up. He's got
bushy thick eyebrows.
Frame wide, round brown eyes.
Nose shaped arrow-like.
Full lips, plump and slobbering.

Look like him...

Is him.
Where's your gun?

IN MY CLOSET

How you beg for a gun?
But ain't carrying one?
Jada!

Land-Lord calls,
He puts her gun in my hand.
He hands Jada his iPhone.

Jada, roll some video!

She records.

Wake him!

Pirate lifts a bucket.
Water pours.
Dude coughs, kicks, shivers.

Fool, you killed her daddy!
On the court.
He turns to me.
Take your shot.   .

Just, like that?

Yes. What else you need?
Engraved invitation?

DUDE IN THE CHAIR

Start pleading.
Start crying.
Start begging.

Land-Lord says,

> *Next, he gonna be lying.*
> *Raise the gun to your chest.*
> *Grab the trigger.*
> *Bullet do the rest.*

> *Yo, you got this!*
> **Jada tells me,**
> *He spilled your family blood.*
> *Somebody gotta pay.*

Dude start blabbering,
Forgive me!
Have mercy!
Please, please!

SOMETHING DOESN'T FEEL RIGHT

Is he high?
I ask.

Yeah,
Land-Lord says.
Digger and Pirate found him
by a trap house off of Genesee.

Dang,
Heavy-eyed Lou whispers,
A junkie killed your daddy?

Dude starts mumbling.
Wasn't trying...
Just needed money...
Mercy...please...

SHUT UP!
Gag that fool!

Wait!
I say,
I wanna know why he did it.

YOU WANNA KNOW WHY?

Look at that fool.
He's outta his mind.
Why don't matter.
Why
*don't **ever** matter.*

He stole from you!
You giving forgiveness?
Think it was an accident?

Remember what he did?
He stepped up
*to **YOUR** daddy.*
Raised his gun.
Shot him.
Point blank.
No warning.

No prisoners.
No mercy.

HE GRABS MY HAND

That hand that holds the gun.
Lifts it toward Dude.

You asked.
I found.
Close the deal.

Pirate and Digger move from the firing
line.
Dude's tear-soaked face
stares at me.
His fear, so pitiful.
Wetting his pants.

A bullet flies above his head.

Alive, he screams.

Dropping the gun,
I run.

LAND-LORD'S VOICE LAUGHS

as I run out of the building.
Jada calls after me.
Hear her voice.
Hear her footsteps.
I cannot stop.
My legs cannot stop.
This is not—
This cannot—

> *Yo! Aaliyah!*
> *Stop, girl!*
> *Come on!*

Jada tackles me to the ground
as we hear a gunshot sing.

> *No prisoners,* Jada says.

HOLD THIS

We go back.
Land-Lord and Jada
exchange gun for iPhone.

*You're a disappointment,
Aaliyah,* **says Land-Lord.**
*Thought you were hard.
Thought you wanted
revenge, girl!
Payback!*

*He was so...
So...*

*Sorry? Pathetic?
That's what happens to fools.
You ain't foolish, are you?
Work hard for results
because your invoice is at
payment due.*

PAYMENT DUE

I had to close the deal,
Land-Lord says.

I didn't tell you to do that!

Land-Lord got answers.
Think I'm gonna just let him go?
Yo, we've gone too far to
turn back now.
That's where this is.
The point of no return.

Now what?

Yeah, alright.
All business.
Figure out how to lose
the championship game
next week.

BETWEEN A ROCK AND A CONCRETE WALL

What?
I can't do that! Why do that?

> *You still stuck on whys?*
> *You know, curiosity*
> *killed the cat.*

He pauses.

> *You need to know.*
> *The McKinley Meteorites lose*
> *the championship.*
> *Or you and me*
> *will have serious problems.*
> *Problems that will get fixed*
> *unfriendly, painfully, and quickly.*
> *We clear?*

DEAD PEOPLE DON'T TALK

There's a gun somewhere,
wearing my fingerprints.
There's a gun somewhere,
whose bullet delivered a death sentence.
There's a gun somewhere.
Could be evidence against me.
There's a gun somewhere.
That fired deadly damages.
There's a gun somewhere
with a story to tell.
Hardened with steel.
Could land me in a cell.

I'M UP EARLY

Because I didn't really sleep.
Pull the blanket to Pop's shoulder.
I shower and dress,
make coffee.
The smell stirs Pop awake.

So?
You going to the championship?

Yeah.
I pour him some coffee.

That's all? Yeah?

Slide him the cup.

Yeah.
Not done yet.
Still gotta play it.

GONNA BE THERE, THIS TIME

I will.
This is history, girl!
You know McKinley Meteorites
ain't never got this far before!

Yeah, I know.

I promise, Granma and I both be there!

It's really okay.
It don't really matter.

It does matter!
To everybody.
Your dad...
George...woulda...
we all...
we're all proud of you.

WAITING ON THE CORNER

Land-Lord's Lexus.
His ride doesn't feel
better than the bus
no more.

Today, Land-Lord be that house cat
who got all day just sitting around,
waiting for a mouse.

He doesn't want to kill the mouse.
Just to play with it.
Filled with enough power
to destroy.

I'm the mouse.

HOW YOU FEELING, SHORTY?

Land-Lord says.

Can I ask you something?
I say.

It's a free country.

Why you help me get stronger
if you want me to throw this game?

You can't figure that out?
I'm a businessman.
Everybody love underdogs.
Wanna see them rise.
Wanna believe they're
invincible.
Sports is will,
skill, luck,
game of chance.

ALL GAMES AIN'T PLAY

You played me.

> *This is where we at?*
> *You brought me a list.*
> *Gun, check.*
> *Shooter, check.*
> *Even finished the job for you.*
> *Revenge 101.*
> *You honored your daddy.*
> *Stop whining.*

I ain't whining.
But he's dead.
Did he really do it?

> *It doesn't matter now, does it?*
> *Have a good day at school.*

EIGHT PERIODS
TIL PRACTICE

Moving through the hallways.
Dreamy, nothing's real.

Mouths say,
congratulations.
Cannot even deal.
Open hands pat and bump.

But I'm numb. I'm a rock.
Yesterday went tick-tock.

I'm praying for it back.

Blurring memories in this game.
Dude's face reflecting everywhere.
Dude?
Didn't get his name.
Believed I wouldn't care.

TREATING US LIKE HEROES

All over the school.
Ms. Henderson got
Team Spirit.
Know our team never got this far before.
Ever.
And I know,
I know.
Winning, mad important.
Everyone's showing us,
winning's the most important thing.
Try hiding behind smiles.
A mask for public me.

Dude's tear-filled face,
still steady piercing through me.

LUNCH ROOM TIME-OUT

School's serving cake and ice cream.
Nod to some team.
Spot Jada and Heavy-eyed Lou,
keeping place for me.

What's up?
asks Jada.

I sit myself down.
I don't eat.

Gotta take an L.
Or your man's making me clown.

Memory says, you wanted in this game.
Word is bond
to keep.

POINTS IN THE PAINT

My life is the ball.
      Game title: Self-preservation.
Clock is ticking.
      Think offense
and defense.
      Need another time out
to take the lead.
      Gotta get a turnover.
Keep my footing.
      Stay in bounds.
Get back the ball.
      Be lightning fast.
Finger-roll to the rim.
      Cut and finish.
Make the shot.

NEW PAIR OF ADIDAS

Shoved inside my bag.
Land-Lord says, *Keep it.*

Expensive painkiller swag.

Contract's his terms.
Play with heart.
Give a show.

Until the half's end.

Asks if I'm cool.
Answer yes.
Give Jada dap.
Exit car.

Adjust pack shoulder straps.
Focus straight ahead.

Pop-Pop stands at sidewalk cracks.
Shaking his head.

WHAT BUSINESS YOU GOT

inside that man's car?
Don't know what you doing,
but know who you are.

He's a born troublemaker.
From skin to bone.
Destroying peace, double talking.
Imitating stars.

Dad and him was tight,
back in the day?
Friends, right?
I ask.

Until betrayal.
Easy money schemes.

Gave Georgie prison.
Taking his dreams.

POP-POP'S PLEA

Been stumbling, been tripping,
Been sliding, been slipping,
Been falling, been crying.
Done bawling,

about trying.

You got courts to rule
Got hoops to smash.
Got nets to cut loose.

Don't be fooled by flash.

Your dreams coming true.

Let's both
get out these streets.

Cause I'm here for you.

GO AHEAD, BET
AGAINST ME

What am I gonna do?
Play without heart?
Make us lose?
Nobody will really know...

They'll say:

Too bad McKinley lost.
Double-A sure was looking off.

Then go about their day.

Coach'll give a speech
about accepting defeat.
Girls gonna scream, curse, cry.

But afterward,
can I live with myself?

CHAMPIONS GET CROWNED

Coach starts her speech.
Hyping us all up.
Zenning us down.

> *Ladies, today marks history.*
> *For you,*
> *this team,*
> *and the school.*
> *You have already made us*
> *so very proud.*
> *The war isn't over.*
> *We have one last battle to win!*
>
> *Play with heart and take that crown!*

WELCOME TO THE GIRLS BASKETBALL METRO CHAMPIONSHIP

Everyone's here.
Just like they promised.
Granma, Pop-Pop, Bobby, Ms. Sheree.
Even Ms. Henderson
got her school colors on.

So much hope.
So much pride.
For championship.

Left side of the court,
Pirate and Digger.
Right side,
Jada and Heavy-eyed Lou.
Don't see Land-Lord.
But I know,
he's lurking,
Somewhere.

HALFTIME

The score 20–35,
City Honors.
Down by fifteen points?
McKinley doesn't look too good,
Mia.

> *Yes, Leah.*
> *Coach Barron replaced*
> *Lindsay Warren, the end of the first*
> *with Aaliyah Davis.*
> *But "Double-A"*
> *isn't making the grade!*

She'd better find her heart
soon,
or City Honors will celebrate
this championship win.

A TIME-OUT

Coach starts reading me.

You're all over the place!

What's going on?

Focus,
Aaliyah!
We need you!
Get in this GAME!

Her eyes,
microscoping into my fears.

We got each other.
We got you.
We're here together.
YOU gotta LEAD on that floor!
I know you got this!
You GOT THIS!

THE FINAL COUNT-DOWN

Looking for me.
Looking at me.
Waiting for me
to come through.
Coach believes
teams achieve dreams.
X-ray visioning ability
building callouses on fragility.

Words freestyle through my lips.
Like jump shots.
Gotta make my daddy proud.

Y'all wanna win!?
Why we born?
Make it rain!
Shoot this storm!
What's our name?
You better shout!
MEE-TEE-OR-ITES.

Bring our trophy out!

SIX SECONDS ON THE CLOCK

We're down by five.
Swish!

Now three!
Brianna blocks City Honors.
Two-shot attempt.

Three-second clock.
My ball—
nobody is open!

Cue slow-motion.
Three-point attempt.

Leaping, lifting, lining up,
Laser-eyes on basket.
Ball releases.
Flees, floats, flies, flows.
Buzzer bleats, beeps,
screams, screeches.

Game over.
We're champions!

SOUND LIKE THUNDER

Applause, excitement,
joy, and tears.
We're jumping and hugging!

There are my grandparents.
Standing,
cheering, clapping.

There,
behind Granma,
Land-Lord's face.
Pop-Pop doesn't see him.

He's stares me down.
He waves.
His hand mimics
a gun.

Pointer finger straight at me.
Thumb pulled back.
His lips mouth one word,
Pow.

WORRIED WINNER'S WEEKEND

Been deep on guard.
Every hour, every day.
Another shoe gonna drop.
Another act of pain.

When we won,
        hand motioning a gun.
Out there,
        creeping.

Which direction is he coming from?

Could be tomorrow,
next week,
or today.

Target on my back.
So my gun is stashed
in my backpack,
protection before any attack.

BACK AT SCHOOL

At the locker,
my bag's going inside.
Heavy-eyed Lou,
up my nose,
my back-pack thud,
triggering
Heavy-eyed Lou's question.

You packing?

Cold stare.

You better.

Eyeing my backpack,

Seen Jada?

Nah.

She ran away.
Gone.
You should run too,
or hide.
Land-Lord for real.
Your championship win
messed with his money.

INCOME STREAMS

Land-Lord took bets on the game.
Odds were in favor of McKinley.
He bet lots on City Honors,
against you.

You take the L,
he makes buckets
of duckets.

Everybody else bets on McKinley.
Losers.
But
you didn't obey,
Land-Lord had to pay.
And so, well.
Here we are,
today.

RIGHT BEFORE LUNCH

Loudspeaker
calls me to the office.
Principal Bennett walks me
to my locker.
My heart pushing
against my chest.

A police officer stands.
The school super,
Mr. Griffin, cuts my lock.

Principal Bennett
unzips my backpack.
Eyes spotlight the contents.
Eyes jumping up to mine.

Showing anger, fright, and shock.

CONSEQUENCES

I didn't cry.
I didn't squeal.
I shut down.

I'm arrested.
I'm a minor.
There's a process.
Criminal possession of a loaded gun.
Unlicensed, unregistered.

Heavy-eyed Lou
dropped Land-Lord the intel?

The gun's in her locker.

Pop-Pop tries getting me home.
But court says
I'm going to County Youth Detention.

NEW KID IN TOWN

I've never been a punk.
Never been a
bully or a jerk.

I'm a jock,
bit of a clown.
Popular Crew member.

In high school,
found my people,
found my team.

But the world,
in this life,
got different rules,
cutthroat scenes.

Survival of the fittest
by any necessary means.

THE COUNTY YOUTH DETENTION CENTER

Court-ordered temporary secured facility.
What this is:
my new home
until the county looks at,
reads, talks to...?
In order to learn:

> *Where'd you get the gun?*
> *Why'd you bring it to school?*
> *Any ballistic results?*
> *Interview her teachers, parents.*
> *Psychological review.*

Wow, what'd I get myself into?

DETENTION'S LIKE SCHOOL

If it wasn't for:

all the girls wearing
the same dark blue
stiff-cotton jumpsuit.
Tan-brown rubber flip-flops.
White cotton socks.

Guess
it's like school.

Like, a *really* messed up
boarding school or something.

Like, a nicer orphanage
than in that book *Oliver Twist*.

Shoot...
there's nothing better than being
inside your *real* home.

FOR YOUR PROTECTION

Guards at every door.
Guards for walking escorts.
Guards in classrooms
with teachers.
Guards in the cafeteria.
Guards watching camera monitors.
Guards watching over us in the pods.

Pod = individual, locked "bedrooms"
we sleep in.
Or
get timed-out in.

Guards, cameras, steel bars, steel locks,
and steel doors.

MY BODY'S TOO LONG

for this bed.
My feet hang down.
So, I bend up my knees.
My body's too long
for this bed.
My head hangs over.
So, I bend my head down.
My body is too long
for this bed.
No pillow provided.
So, my bent neck
rests on my forearm.

Goodnight.

RECREATION TIME

There's always somebody,
Jack or Jill.
They don't like to ball.
They don't know how?
Not willing to work?
Then there's the
wannabe player.
Talk good game.
Knows plays and names.
But ain't got real game.
Then they're those
who play ball with
skill, finesse.
No brags.
No mess.
Just swish.
Yes!

CHRISTINE

is a bruiser.
Meaning she'll hurt you
without thought.

Not realizing
how strong she is.
Those weaker
get caught

within her grip.
Under her foot.
Her elbow really
smarts.

I'm gonna call for Christine
next time
they take us to the gym.
She will be there
to foul and block.

LASHONDRA

Comes from Cheektowaga,
where the airport lives.
We were game opponents once.
LaShondra got game to give.

Ran with Cheektowaga Central High.
She complains too much.
Gets fouled and starts fights.
But I'll get as rough as rough.

Knowing about strategy,
LaShondra's game
don't scare me.
I know how I'm made.

CLOSING IN ON ME

They could plan to
try me,
play me,
or
test me.
Push up on me
and guess me.

To see how I'm made.
To mess with me.

I know who I am.
I know what I've done.

I wish I was dreaming.
But it's as real as I'm seeing.

FEW MORE QUESTIONS

A detective asks.
My lawyer sits close
while I lie answers.

I had it because I found it.
I don't know.
Maybe somebody dropped it.
Brought it to school.
For some protection benefits.
I was scared.
I don't know.
Somebody killed my dad.
Maybe somebody kills me.

People get killed in the daytime.
People get shot in the daytime.
Day and night.

SAW JADA WEARING DARK BLUE

in the gym,
about to go into teams.
I hear a voice
I've memorized
announcing to someone:

You don't wanna play wit me!
My name is Jada!
I'm un-play-wit-able!

We hear someone struggle.
Some huffs, grunts, and pleas.
A few more footsteps
scuffle and run.

Jada yelling,
Get offa me!

MORNING AFTER
THE SCUFFLE

Walking like a pit bull,
Jada uses
every inch of her
five-foot-four frame
of swagger to
broadcast her message:
*Don't even think about
messing with me!*

First impressions are everything here.

Wait for her
to size everybody else
in the room up.
Before noticing me.

Unless she's looking
for me?

YOU LOOKING FOR ME?

Aaliyah! What's up?!

Jada goes for a homegirl greeting,
but we're met with
the violation buzzer.

A red-buttoned ringer
announcing when we young
incarcerates—that's us—
stand too close
to one another.

NO touching!
NO handshakes!
NO claps, no hugs, no high fives!

> *Wanna play Uno?*

Get a table.
I'll deal.

RECAP

Dealing seven cards out.
Red, green, yellow, blue.
Wildcard.

> *You stuck your middle finger up*
> *at Land-Lord,*
> Jada says, so that no one
> else can hear.

He sent you here for me?
I ask.

Her cards face down,
Jada locks eyes.

> *That's what you thinking?*

Don't know what to think.

AIN'T BLOOD THICKER

Shoulda shuffled longer.
Got four reds and three greens.

> *Think I was gonna sacrifice you?*

He's your godfather.
Who you loyal to?
I'm here for a gun at school.
He gave you something
to hold over me.
What I'm supposed to think?

Red skip, reverse, draw four.
Skip, reverse, Uno!

HALF-EMPTY

Under normal circumstances,
my loyalty would be unquestionable.
Under normal circumstances,
my actions would be toward preservable.

Normal circumstances changed,
while discovering I feel for you.
Normal circumstances changed
after uncovering my heart just grew.

The more I know,
the more I grow.
I've grown some more,
I'm trying to say.

I KNEW

when you won the game,
he won't never ever let that go.
Didn't know how else
to keep you safe.
So, I told Lou,
text me when he thought
you were geared up
and packed.

But he called Land-Lord.
He told the cops.

There's some more
you need to know.

YOUTH DETENTION WORKER

Jada Green!
Time for you to visit the social worker.

Jada leaves the table with Miss Barbara,
a youth detention worker.
A nice, long title for:
Juvenile Jail Guard.

Miss Barbara is nice enough.
I don't have no beef with her.
Interested in what Jada had to
say to me.

NEW GIRL

I'm shocked to see her
here.

Her name's Shanequa,
I say to Mariah.
Mariah's all up in Shanequa's face,
being nosy, asking questions.
I know Mariah tryna make a new friend,
but Shanequa scared as a rabbit.
She ain't about detention life.
Guess anyone can end up here.

Leave her alone, Mariah!

    Huh?

You all up in her face.
Let her breathe some air.

    Why, my breath stinks?

Yes! Go brush your teeth!

152

THE SMARTEST GIRL IN THE HOOD

Last time I saw you, Shanequa,
you was my fake tutor, **I say.**
What you do,
steal library books at your private school?

She don't laugh.
She scared seriously straight.

> *I got in a fight at school.*
> *Broke a girl's nose.*

Word, didn't know you had it in you!
Don't be afraid, a'ight?
I won't let nobody mess with you.

I got her back.

That's what it means
to be part
of the same team.

IN GROUP THERAPY

One day Dad and I were happy.
Laughing at plays.
Blink my eyes,
watch him die one day.

One day, Dad and I were watching
the Clippers game.
Next at his funeral,
forgetting people's names.

One day the sky was cloudless blue.
Today it's stone gray.
Rain is falling, too.

HOW DOES THAT MAKE YOU FEEL?

The person in charge of
group therapy session
named Miss Esther.
Samantha likes her shoes.
Jada called her pretty.
She isn't from Buffalo.
Miss Esther from
New York City.

She asks me how I'm feeling.
Since I saw Dad shot dead.

How I feel?
*How you **think** I feel!?*

I DON'T KNOW

That's why I'm asking.
Do you know what you feel?
Can you name those feelings?

Name them?

I'm angry.
I'm mad.
I'm unhappy.

I'm sad.
Been quiet.
I feel blue.
Having nightmares,
in the daytime, too.

Granma   don't like   the   words:

"Dad is dead."
Grandpop drinks,

slowing anger in his head.

WE GO AROUND IN A CIRCLE

Miss Esther makes everybody talk
especially when they don't want to.
Christine ain't the one trying to
hide her anger.
Don't make her, no never mind
who sees her.
She'll cry and scream.
Tears washing all over her face.
In her pod, she wrestles dreams
cause she thinks somebody
punching her face.

JADA AND MISS ESTHER

Jada says her trauma started
when she was a little girl.
She thinks it was a curse,
her coming in this world.
Since her daddy died
on her birthday.
Holding her cake.
She steady blames herself
for his murder
that day.

Saying if she wasn't born,

he'd be alive today.

LASHONDRA
AND JADA

got beef grilling and growing.
They both got anger issues.
Got winds of tension blowing.

Jada ain't ever one for backing from a fight.

Staring her down
is an interpretation
of an invitation

to throw up hands and throw down.

LaShondra bored, she needs attention.

She just wants to play.

WORLD MIGHTA BEEN BETTER

Jada was wide open
for LaShondra's remark.
What you say?

> Miss Esther says,
> *LaShondra, group is a*
> *safe place.*
> *We respect one another here.*

> LaShondra shrugs,
> *Whatever.*

Nah,
says Jada.
I asked a simple question.
*What you **say**?*

> Miss Esther tries to squash
> the fire.
> *Ladies! Let's just—*

LaShondra says,
I said, world woulda been better if you
switched with your daddy!

A FIGHT! A FIGHT!

Before the fight
goes down,
feel the excitement of a fight.
Feel the thrill of a strike!
My eyes getting wide.
Blood pressure going high!
The rush is feeling bright.
We know it's wrong,
but it feeling right!

When she fights,
Jada's part Spanish bull,
ready to strike.
Running straight through
her opponent.
Bent over from her waist.
Two feet, scratch the floor back.
Like she's readying her pace.

Jada's head like a fast-running bullet.
LaShondra's gonna haveta learn today
after Jada hits her gullet!

THAT'S HOW YOU GET ISOLATED

Isolation for fighting.
The most popular violation.

Ain't gonna lie,
when it was Jada's turn talking,
I saw LaShondra
making faces, smirking.
Now she on her way
to the hospital.

Jada prolly just
changed her life
though.

LaShondra won't never
make fun of somebody
she doesn't know,
ever again.

JADA, CHRISTINE, MARIAH, SHANEQUA, & ME

Got separate paths.
Separate pains.
Separate therapies.

Jada in isolation again
for another fight, with Christine.

But I'm copying Daddy
like when he was locked down.
Writing my lyrics,
adjusting my crown.
Dad had a choice—
gangster or legit.
Find that table,
know where you sit.

Been writing out verses.
Shanequa makes beats.
Mariah watches us work.
We sounding and feeling free!
Making friends beyond Jada.
Refocus, reframe my dreams.
A champion, not a player,
who's changing into me!

POP-POP VISITS

Your Granma, she in the car.
I'm supposed to call her when we done.

She's not coming inside to see me?

> *She'll be in here when you*
> *and me done.*

How is she?

> *You really got her good.*
> *After we got the call,*
> *your granmama ain't been*
> *that quiet since*
> *I don't know when.*
> *Pretending like you just run away.*
>
> *Now what's this all about, Aaliyah?*
> *Is it true?*
> *You really bring a gun to school?*
> *Why? This is serious.*
> *People could get hurt.*

Thought...I sorta...needed it.
Thought, I was feeling kinda scared.
Don't know, I don't know.

Don't know what I was thinking.
Just wanna come home.

GRANMA'S VISIT

What did I do wrong with you?
Why do you and your father insist
on circling around
the darkness of those streets!

Just what is wrong?
Huh?
What did we do wrong?

Maybe I should have let your mama
take you back to Atlanta
after George passed.

I don't know.

HE'S DEAD

Dad is dead, Granma.
He didn't pass by anything.
He didn't pass over anything.
He didn't pass through,
under, over
anything, anyone, or anyplace!

George Davis Jr.
is dead!
Shot.
Three times
in the chest.
By somebody
who probably
didn't even know his real name.

He was murdered, killed!
Dead!

GRANMA LEAVES

the room crying.
Big, loud, awful tears.
I didn't mean to speak like that.
I didn't mean to yell.
I couldn't hold it back.
The boiling point just swelled.
My voice just could not be still.
Felt like that copper water kettle
Granma keeps on our stove.
Screaming until it spills over.

SPECIAL VISITOR

Some of us get more visits
than others.
Typical visits allowed include
your parents or guardians.
Your lawyer.
The head person at your church.
Today, it was Coach.
Got me out of science class today.
She got some special permission
through my lawyer or something.

You look alright, Aaliyah.

COACH'S VISIT

For true?
My hair is mad dry.
Have to use the no-lather
state soap.
My skin is ashy.
I lost weight
on account food here don't taste right.
But yeah,
bet I look different
than you imagined,
huh?

I was just—

Yeah, I know.
Making small talk,
I know.

Grown-ups like to do that,
especially here.
What's up,
Coach?

I don't mean to ride you.
I'm glad that you're here.

Thanks.
Then she drops the bomb.

I could be banned from playing
at the high school level.

Even though
I never fired the gun.
Criminal possession, locked and
loaded
in a school building,
that's enough grounds
for the punishment.

I'm fighting for you, Aaliyah.
But I really don't know enough
about why you did it
to defend you being able to stay, yet.

After my case is settled,
the athletic association
will decide my athletic fate.

POP-POP WITH THE LAWYER

They say I have to wait in here
longer.
Until the police department finishes
doing tests.
Checking to see if the gun
was used in another crime.
And the county finishes running
investigations into home,
family, and school life.

The lawyer says,
Courts don't like guns in schools.
So, get comfortable,
stay out of trouble.
The court will take your
stay here into account.
I don't want to scare you, but
it could take a little while.
Gun charges always do.
So, um, are you getting along alright?
Anybody bothering you?
I can make some calls, if you need?
Alright, I'll let you and your granddad talk.

YOU REMEMBER HOW
I TAUGHT YOU

to throw and take a punch,
right?
Pop-Pop asks.
Try not to let these punk
girls scare you.
You got height on your side.
You scared?
They might be scared of you!

He laughs.
I smile.

You're going to have
regular meetings.
Talk with a therapist
about how you feel.

You hungry?

BACK IN GENERAL POPULATION

Jada walking 'round
a little taller than before.
Saying she can take someone
twice her size down to the floor.

Now she can finally tell me
what she had to say.

Jada grabs the backgammon board.
We take a seat to play.
Jada says she hid away
the proof we need to
keep Land-Lord at bay,
keeping us both safe.

JADA'S STORYTIME

Remember when we were
all back inside the warehouse?
The day Land-Lord brought you
to Dude?
Remember he gave me his phone
to make a video?

I used my phone
instead of his.
Cause my intuition
was feeling a quiz.

Never stopped the video
until after we got
back inside his car.

You ran away
before the gunshot.
Innocent!
You were too far!

IN THE VIDEO, I'M HOLDING

I say.

> Yes, but you ran away!
> It's shaky, but you can see me
> running after you.
> You can hear me calling you.
> And
> my tackling you.
> You can hear Land-Lord,
> plain as day,
> saying that he had to finish the job
> because you wouldn't!
> Plus, lots more.
>
> You sure it's safe?

THE FIRST TIME

Haven't been happy in a long time.
Is it true?
Can I—can *we*—be free of Land-Lord's
hold?
Could I start living life like it's new?
Or could this be a trap?
A gangster-fake-friend
trap?
Making me feel Jada can be trustworthy.
Being real friendly to me.

MOM'S VIDEO CALL

Hello? Mom?

> *Aaliyah!*
> *How are you?*

I'm okay.

> *I've been trying to get information*
> *about what exactly is going on.*
> *First, you're a basketball star,*
> *and next I hear you're a terrorist?*

I'm not a terrorist, Mom.
I just—

> *You brought a gun to school?*
> *Why??*
> *A gun to school??*

JUST ANOTHER KID WITH PROBLEMS

Your life can't be that bad?
Can it?

Thought you could
come back here,
live with us,
but...
Don't think that's
going to work.
Wayne got promoted at the dealership.
We're selling the house.
I'm so overwhelmed now!
Dwayne!
Dwayne!
Your sister on video!
Look, its Aaliyah!

Hi, Aaliyah.

DAD ONCE TOLD ME

Information is currency.
Like silver and gold.
Allowing for purchases
your wallet cannot back up.
Laying every card on the table
leaves you open for quick kills.
Or
take your time.
Allow seeds to flourish.
Allow root growin'.
Make plans, strategies, plays.
Defend your goals.
Map your games.

If ballin' ain't your key,
your mind gotta work creatively.

LAND-LORD STORIES

Jada keeps getting cut off,
sharing Land-Lord's mystery,
deep in his business.
Passing secret history.

The dude he killed
tied in the chair
headed one of Land-Lord's
trap-house lairs.

Started mixing product with pleasure.
You know how it goes.
Indebted to Land-Lord
for triple what he owes.

Communications
between Land-Lord and
your dad was coming
was going.
Land-Lord pressed Boogie-G
to persuade
Miss Sheree at the Center
to stop pushing public political problems
she's been flowing since September.
It was interfering with future plans
he was growing.

Your dad
took to lecturing Land-Lord
like in college,
explaining his plan was whack.
And how Miss Sheree
and the Center
were about community power and
knowledge.

I found some receipts.
I hacked into his phone.
Saved and stored some videos.

Now my father is holding them.
Deep down underground, dark and safe.

But we need another person
we can trust
to get it and
use it on a case
for us.

IT TAKES TWO

This is a terrible tale
Jada's telling.
Giving me
mixed feelings.
Voicing an inner dread.
Jada naming Land-Lord
as the one causing my
Dad's death.

I shoulda known!
Did I reject it?
Could I have accepted?
Feel fooled,
twisted, and chumped.
Land-Lord was prolly laughing
at making me his punk.

Dad would be
disappointed
and ashamed
seeing his prodigy
move in the
opposite direction
his bricks were
paving.
But my destiny is shiny.
It takes the lead,
in my opinion.
Not bowing or pleading
like somebody's minion.

Land-Lord's the villain
I have to slay.
I choose to do it
the Boogie-G way.

TO GET
POP-POP'S HELP

means telling him the truth.
The whole truth, the entire truth,
and nothing but the truth.
Also means him keeping
the promise to follow the plan.
Including not going up
and approaching the man.

We cannot let Land-Lord have
any little itty-bitty bit
of an upper hand.
Practice cool, quiet,
closed-mouthed-ness.

Stealth with each action.
Disguising our plans
to bring Land-Lord's
falsely protected world
tumbling right down.
Locking him deep down
below the jail.

POP-POP LISTENED

without cutting me off.
His face tells me what
he is thinking
and feeling.
Pop-Pop listens to my story
of the gun
and all that follows.
I see his fear,
haunted by wonder,
shadowing his disgust,
trailing behind surprise,
tracking his anger.

Speaking clear and steady,

What do you need me to do?

JADA HID THE EVIDENCE

in the cemetery, close
to her father's grave.
Wrapping gun and telephone
in Ziplock bags and tape.
Burying them deep underground,
keeping the contents safe.

Pop-Pop spoke to the lawyer.
The lawyer got
the district attorney.
The attorney got the police.
The police dug the evidence.
Bringing it to the court.

Police said for the past
eight years or so,
they've been
building a Land-Lord case.
Whenever they get close,
he always slips away.
They search the trails of his
illegal organized businesses.
But their proof
lands in the court like bricks.
Jada's given them
the strongest evidence.
These charges will definitely stick.

HOMEWARD BOUND

Jada and me,
going home!
The judge saw and
heard the evidence.
Now Jada and me getting set free.
We both got to testify against him.
That makes Jada a little uneasy.
She's steady afraid of the homies.

Gonna call her out for being a rat,
informer, traitor, punk, or squeal.

You know,
reputation is all some folks
in the world got.
Where we from,
people have a hard time
trusting somebody
if you didn't have your peep's back
during an important moment.
Know what I mean?
But then again,
we have to be able to recognize
if having someone's back
within that moment,
means your own back is
gonna get bruised, bent,
broke, or cracked.

Is that moment a benefit for you?
Is it a sacrifice you can afford?
Do the consequences seem true?
Is it worthy of your heart?

Is your crew ride and fly?
Helping you reach and dream?

Or are you a
ride and die
ready to sacrifice for
screams.
Friends want you to be the best
you want to be!
Know what I mean?

ONE GRANDMOTHER

My mother's mother
died before my birth.
One grandmother I have
on the earth.
When I return,
Granma cooks roast,
macaroni and cheese,
greens, and pie.
My bed made
with favorite pillows.

I apologize for yelling.

She hugs me tight.
Pulls me in,
kissing my cheek.
Saying, *I love you,
alright.*

CAN I PLAY OR
IS IT NO?

My phone ring-rings.
Coach on the line.
Talking about future things:
the athletic association
decided my fate.
One year suspension
for next year's 11th grade.
They'll review my case
before 12th grade begins.
Look me over, out and in.

Been writing with Shanequa
these days,
learning how I can
honor my daddy's life
the right way.

Life got different,
since writing with pens.
Poems, rhymes, and lyrics,
got me questioning everything.
Exchange my orange ball
for an empty writing book.
When I fill it?
Y'all be shook!

MY RIDE AND FLY

Had doubts about Jada.
Had bouts with Jada.
Convinced she was against me
even though she was with me.
She took big chances
getting Land-Lord for me.
Got big courage,
big will to be free.
Jada's my girl,
best friend,
my ride and fly!
Gonna figure life out.
Shoot the storm.
Reach for the sky!

I'M THE DOUBLE A-

L-I-Y-A-H.
Been through some things
and seen some aches.
Life is full of choices.
Left. Right. Up. Down.
I stand hearing voices
harmonize within sound.
Mistakes are hard lessons
reflecting your life.
Breathe in deep.
Let it out.
Flip the switch.
Be the light.

WANT TO KEEP READING?

If you liked this book, check out another
book from West 44 Books:

RISING OUT
BY M. AZMITIA

ISBN: 9781978595439

♀
The first time I
saw Eri,

tumbling
onto the grass at
the park near our
homes,

she was a boy
named Maurice.

She screamed as
she fell.

    The Band-Aid
across her nose was
too light.

    Tan on deep, dark
brown skin.

CHECK OUT MORE BOOKS AT:
www.west44books.com

An imprint of Enslow Publishing

WEST **44** BOOKS™

ABOUT THE AUTHOR

Annette Daniels Taylor is the award-winning author of the YA novel-in-verse *Dreams on Fire*. She uses multiple media disciplines, poetry, performance, filmmaking, playwriting, and vocals to tell her stories. A veteran teaching artist, Annette leads writing, performance, and media workshops in various learning institutions and community organizations. Annette is an adjunct professor at SUNY Buffalo State teaching Broadcast Media Writing. Born and raised in Staten Island, Daniels Taylor works and lives with her family, cats, and plants in Buffalo, New York.